# The Nativity Blessing

YOUTHFUL READS
PUBLISHING

Age
3-6

# This book belongs to:

..............................................

..............................................

Age 3-6

Once upon a time, in a cozy little town called Nazareth our story starts.

In Nazareth, there lived a sweet and caring young lady named Mary. She was always there to lend a hand to her mom and dad and to all her neighbors.

Everyone in town held Mary dear in their hearts, and God had a special place for her in His, too.

Soon, Mary was going to marry Joseph, a very nice and honest man.

But just before that, someone very special visited her.

It was Angel Gabriel, dressed in a robe as white as the clouds and had large, shiny wings like the silver moon.

He came from the sky, sent by God.

The Angel spoke gently, "Mary, there's no need to be scared! I've come with wonderful news from God! You're going to have a baby boy. He will be known as the Son of God and the one who will bring hope to everyone. You will call him Jesus."

Mary heard the Angel's words and replied with a brave heart, "I believe in God's plan! May everything happen just as God has chosen!"

During one starry night, while Joseph was dreaming, the Angel came to visit his dream.

The Angel said, "Joseph! I bring a message from God. Mary will have a baby, and this child is blessed and will be known as the Son of God!"

Joseph embraced this heavenly news and, a few days afterward, he married Mary.

During that time, the ruler of the land decided to count all the people, which meant Mary and Joseph had to make their way to Bethlehem.

Their journey was long and hard, and for Mary, who was very close to having her baby, it was even more challenging.

She sat carefully on a donkey's back, with Joseph guiding them step by step.

Once they reached Bethlehem, Mary and Joseph found that all the inns were full, with no room for them to rest.

The only spot they could find was a cozy corner in a barn where animals snuggled in for the night.

As the night fell silent, a miracle unfolded. Mary brought into the world a precious baby boy named Jesus. Together, Mary and Joseph tucked him into a manger for his first sweet sleep, with animals nearby as his first gentle friends.

Mary's heart was full of joy, for the Angel's words had become real. In a simple manger, Jesus Christ, the one who would bring great love to the world, was born.

A little way from Bethlehem, a group of shepherds were watching over their sheep when, out of nowhere, an Angel appeared to them.

The Angel reassured them, "There's no need to fear! I've come to tell you a wonderful story - Jesus has been born! Look for him, and you'll find him resting in a manger!"

Filled with excitement about the arrival of the Savior, the shepherds scurried into the town searching for baby Jesus.

As they came upon the Holy Family, they knelt down with awe in the presence of baby Jesus.

Three wise men journeyed across the sandy desert on their camels. Out of the blue, a star shone so brightly in the sky.

They understood right away that it was a sign a special king had come into the world.

For several days, the three wise men journeyed on, guided by the star that gleamed above, until it paused above the manger. They all bowed gently before Jesus.

To honor him as a unique king, the Son of God, and the one who would bring hope to the world, they offered him royal gifts: gold, frankincense, and myrrh, treasures usually reserved for the greatest of kings.

And that's the tale of the very first Christmas, the beginning of the Savior's journey here on Earth.

He arrived to fill our lives with

Love, Joy, Peace, and Hope!

# Thank you for reading!

Share the joyous spirit of Christmas with your little ones this holiday season!

Let them learn that Jesus came to spread cheer, kindness, and love to everyone. And guess what? Even now, as it was 2,000 years ago, Jesus continues to perform wonders and guides children and adults all around the world!

# We'd like to know what you think!

If you could take a moment to share your thoughts in a review, we would greatly appreciate it!

## YOUTHFUL READS
PUBLISHING

Designed by educators for educators and caregivers.
Ideal for preschools, kindergartens, educational homeschooling, Sunday schools, families, and beyond.